To Michael, David, and Chrissy – who love to wreak
havoc while Mom and Dad Snore On
– KW

For Alan Baker, my tutor
– JC

SIMON AND SCHUSTER
First published in Great Britain in 2001 by Simon & Schuster UK Ltd
1st Floor, 222 Gray's Inn Road, London, WC1X 8HB
A CBS COMPANY

This edition published in 2012 for Index Books

Originally published in 2001 by Pocket Books, an imprint of Simon & Schuster Inc., New York

Text copyright © 2001 by Karma Wilson
Illustrations copyright © 2001 Jane Chapman
All rights reserved.

The rights of Karma Wilson and Jane Chapman to be identified as the author and illustrator of this work
have been asserted by them in accordance with the Copyright, Designs and Patents Act, 1988

All rights reserved including the right of reproduction in whole or in part in any form.

Book design by Ann Bobco.
The text for this book is set in Adobe Caslon.
The illustrations are rendered in acrylic paint.

A CIP catalogue record for this book is available from the British Library upon request.

ISBN: 978-0-85707-670-0

Printed in China

1 3 5 7 9 10 8 6 4 2

Bear Snores On

Karma Wilson

illustrations by Jane Chapman

SIMON AND SCHUSTER

*I*n a cave, in the woods in his deep, dark lair, through the long, cold winter sleeps a great brown bear.

Cuddled in a heap, with his eyes shut tight,
he sleeps through the day, he sleeps through
the night.

The cold winds howl and the night sounds growl.

But
the bear
snores on.

An itty-bitty mouse-pitter-pat, tip-toe-creep-crawls
in the cave from the fluff-cold snow.

Mouse squeaks, "Too damp, too dank, too dark." So he lights wee twigs with a small, hot spark.

The coals pip-pop and the wind doesn't stop.

But
the bear
snores on.

Two glowing eyes sneak-peek in the den.
Mouse cries, "Who's there?" and a hare hops in.

"Ho Mouse!" says Hare. "Long time, no see!" So they pop white corn. And they brew black tea.

Mouse sips wee slurps. Hare burps big BURPS!

But
the bear
snores on.

A badger scuttles by, sniff-snuffs at the air.
"I smell yummy-yums! Perhaps we can share?

"I've brought honey-nuts," Badger says with a grin.
"Let's divvy them up, cosy down . . . and dig in!"

And they nibble and they munch with a

CHEW–

CHOMP–

CRUNCH!

But
the bear
snores on.

A gopher and a mole tunnel up through the floor.
Then a wren and a raven flutter in through the door!

Mole mutters, "What a night!"
"What a storm!" twitters Wren.
And everybody clutters in the great bear's den.

They tweet and they titter. They chat and they chitter.

But
the bear
snores on.

*I*n a cave, in the woods, a slumbering bear
sleeps through the party in his very own lair.

Hare stokes the fire. Mouse seasons stew.

Then a small pepper fleck makes the bear . . .

R A A A A A - C H O O

He blows and he sneezes,
and the whole crowd freezes . . .

And
the bear
WAKES UP!

BEAR GNARLS

and SNARLS.

BEAR ROARS

and he RUMBLES!

BEAR JUMPS

and he STOMPS.

BEAR GROWLS

and he GRUMBLES!

"you've sneaked into my lair
and you've all had fun!
but me? I was sleeping
and ...

I've had none!"

And he whimpers and he
moans, he wails and he groans ...

And the bear blubbers on!

Mouse squeaks, "Don't fret. Don't fuss. Look, see? We can pop more corn! We can brew more tea!"

Bear gulps. Bear gobbles. He sighs with
delight. Then he spins tall tales through
the blustery night.

When the sun peeks up on a crisp
clear dawn . . . Bear can't sleep,

But
his friends
snore on.